Miss McKee

Ready-to-Read

WORTHINGTON BOTTS
AND THE
STEAM MACHINE

By Betty Baker

Pictures by Sal Murdocca

Macmillan Publishing Co., Inc., New York

With thanks to

Phyllis Larkin, who told me how she read when she walked to school, and

Prof. George Moore, who built a steam man in 1890

—B. B.

To Ruth

—S. M.

Macmillan Publishing Co., Inc., 866 Third Avenue, New York, N.Y. 10022. Collier
Macmillan Canada, Ltd. Printed in the United States of America. LIBRARY OF CONGRESS
CATALOGING IN PUBLICATION DATA: Baker, Betty. Worthington Botts and the steam
machine. (Ready-to-read) SUMMARY: In the 1890's, Worthington Botts builds a steam-
powered robot to help him with his chores so he will have more time to read. [1.
Reading—Fiction. 2. Robots—Fiction] I. Murdocca, Sal. II. Title. PZ7.B1693Wo
1981 [E] 80-24627 ISBN 0-02-708190-7   10 9 8 7 6 5 4 3 2 1

Worthington Botts
always said,
"If somebody wrote it,
I can know it."
And Worthington wanted
to know everything.
His friends said
he already knew a lot.
He knew how to make
a lean-to of logs,
how to fix a clock
or stuff an owl.
He could also
play baseball.

But whatever he did,
he tried to read
at the same time.
"Worthington Botts,"
his friends yelled,
"stop reading those cans!
You have to watch
for the ball."
"The ball never comes
this far," said Worthington.
"It will," said his friends.
"It will when we play
the Tufftown Nine.
You have to watch!"

But Worthington Botts
went on reading.
He read when he walked,
and drivers yelled,
"Worthington Botts,
get out of the road!
You are going to get
stepped on some day."

He read when he ate,
when he pumped water
and when he weeded
his mother's garden.
"Worthington Botts,"
his mother yelled,
"stop reading that book
and look what you're doing!"
"I can't stop reading,"
Worthington told her.
"There are too many things
I don't know."

He tried to read
when he milked the cow.
But the cow mooed
and tried to kick him.
Then one day
Worthington read
about a steam machine.
It looked like a man
and walked like one.
It could pull carts
and open doors.
The book had drawings
of how it worked.
"I could make that,"
said Worthington Botts.

Then he said, "I will!
My steam machine
will pump water
and pull weeds
and milk the cow
and lead me down
the side of the road.
Then nobody will yell
when I try to read."

15

His friends said,
"Will it play baseball?"
"Why not?" said Worthington Botts.
"Then we can beat
  the Tufftown Nine!"
  said his friends.

And they stopped
playing baseball
and helped to find
stovepipes and wheels,
wires and forks,
bottles and cans
and anything else
Worthington Botts needed
to make the steam machine.
Worthington Botts
didn't have time
to do any reading.
"But I will," he said.
"After I make
   the steam machine."

The steam machine
was seven feet tall
with a pot hat
for a chimney.
Worthington Botts made a fire
inside the machine
and sat down to wait.
Smoke came out of the hat.
His friends said,
"When will it walk?"
"When steam comes out
of its pipe,"
said Worthington Botts.
"There it comes!"
they yelled.

Worthington got up.
He pushed this
and turned that.
The steam machine
began to walk.
Everybody cheered.
"Now I can read,"
said Worthington Botts.
The steam machine
walked to the pump.
(Clang, bang,
whistle and creak.)
It pumped water.
(Whish, whoosh
and a puff of steam.)

It took the pail
to the house.
(Rickety, rackety.)
But it could not walk
up the steps.
(Crash, bang
and lots of steam.)
The water put out
the fire inside.
It took all day
to dry out
the steam machine
and oil it.

Worthington didn't
have time to read.
"But I will," he said,
"when the steam machine
weeds the garden."
The steam machine
pulled the weeds
(whish, whoosh)
and the peas and the beans
and went on (rickety, rack)
into the roses.
"Worthington Botts,"
his mother yelled,
"get that thing
out of my garden!"

Worthington had
to fix the garden.
He could not read
at all that day.
"But I will tomorrow,"
he said,
"when the steam machine
milks the cow."
But the cow didn't like
the whistle and creak.
She mooed and kicked
the steam machine.

Worthington had
to fix its legs.
He could not read
that day, either.

"But I will tomorrow,"
he said, "when I go
to play baseball
with the Tufftown Nine."

He tied a rope
around his waist.
He tied the other end
to the steam machine
so it could lead him
down the side of the road.
The road turned.
The steam machine did not.
It went on.
(Clang, bang
and a puff of steam.)
Worthington Botts
had to go with it.

He slid and bumped
and got stung by bees
before he got free
of the steam machine.
His leg hurt
and his book was lost.

37

But he got to the road
and went on to the game.
His friends yelled,
"Worthington Botts!
Where is the steam machine?"
"I don't know
and I don't care,"
he told them.
"I haven't read anything
since I made it
and now I've lost a book."
"And we'll lose the game
without the steam machine.
You have to find it
right away!" said his friends.

It was too late.
(Clang, bang,
whistle and creak.)
Down the road
came the Tufftown Nine.
The steam machine
walked with them.
"What will we do?"
said Worthington's friends.
"Play ball!" the umpire said.
"Don't worry," Worthington
told his friends.
"That steam machine
hasn't worked right yet.
And I'll watch for the ball.
I promise!"

41

A circus poster
was on the fence,
but Worthington didn't read it.
The Tufftown Nine
had a man on base.
Tin cans rolled by,
but Worthington didn't
stop them and read them.
Now three men were on base.
The steam machine
clanked up to bat.
A newspaper blew
up to Worthington's leg.
He stepped on it
to hold it down.

43

"Strike one!" said the umpire,
and then, "Strike two!"
Worthington bent over
to read the paper.
"Worthington Botts!"
his friends yelled.
"The ball! The ball!"
Worthington looked up
just in time.
"Out!" said the umpire.
But the steam machine
had started to run.

Soon the Tufftown Nine
were running, too.
"Help!" they yelled.
Worthington Botts
threw the ball.
He threw it at
the steam machine's leg
and broke the place
he had fixed.
The steam machine
ran faster and faster.

But the circle it ran in
got smaller and smaller.
Then the other leg broke
and it fell over
(WHOOSH!)
in a cloud of steam.
"Play ball!" said the umpire.
But the Tufftown Nine
had run away.

They didn't come back.
"That means you win,"
the umpire said.
Worthington's friends
began to cheer.
"Worthington Botts,"
they told him,
"your steam machine
worked just fine!
Now can you make it
play hockey?"

"Yes, but I won't,"
said Worthington Botts.
"A steam machine
is too much work.
All I did was fix it.
I'm not going
to fix it again."
He took it home
and put it in the barn.
Without the legs
it was just right
to hold a book.

While Worthington Botts
milked the cow,
he read about a man
who made a balloon.
And pictures showed
how the balloon was made.

BETTY BAKER is the author of outstanding books for children of all ages. Her stories for younger readers include *Latki and the Lightning Lizard*, *Three Fools and a Horse*, *Santa Rat* and *Dupper*. Among her books for older children are *The Great Desert Race*, *Settlers and Strangers*, *The Spirit is Willing* and *A Stranger and Afraid*. She has twice won the Western Heritage Award for the outstanding Western juvenile book.

SAL MURDOCCA has illustrated many popular children's books, including *The Big Cheese* by Eve Bunting, *The Bean Boy* and *Strong John* by Joan Chase Bowden, *Striding Slippers* by Mirra Ginsburg and *1000 Monsters* by Alan Benjamin. He is also the author-illustrator of *The Hero of Hamblett*.